TEACHER'S PET

**Look for these
and other books about
Karen Brewer and her friends
in the
Baby-sitters Little Sisters series**

Jannie, Bobby, Tammy, Sara
Ian, Leslie, Hank, Terri
Nancy, Omar, Audrey, Chris, Ms. Colman
Karen, Hannie, Ricky, Natalie

THE KIDS IN
MS. COLMAN'S CLASS

TEACHER'S PET
Ann M. Martin

Illustrations by Charles Tang

A
LITTLE APPLE
PAPERBACK

SCHOLASTIC INC.
New York Toronto London Auckland Sydney

No part of this publication may be reproduced in whole or in part, or stored in a retrieval system, or transmitted in any form or by any means, electronic, mechanical, photocopying, recording, or otherwise, without written permission of the publisher. For information regarding permission, write to Scholastic Inc., 555 Broadway, New York, NY 10012.

ISBN 0-590-26215-7

12 11 10 9 8 7 6   8 9/9 0/0

Printed in the U.S.A.   40

First Scholastic printing, September 1995

*This book is in honor
of the birth of
Miranda Jensen*

BACK TO SCHOOL

"Nancy! Rise and shine! Time for school!"

Nancy Dawes rolled over. She opened one eye. She glared at her father. "Do I really have to go to school?" she asked.

"Today?" said Mr. Dawes. "But it is Tuesday, the first day of school. Of course you do." He pulled the window shade and let it snap up.

Nancy waited until her father had left her room. "School stinks," she said. "Second grade stinks. Ms. Colman stinks."

She thought about Martha, her *former* best friend. Meanie-mo Martha. Martha was supposed to have been in Ms. Col-

1

man's class with Nancy. But her family had moved away the week before. To another *state*. Nancy would probably never see her again. And now she had no one special to start second grade with.

Nancy did have other friends. She even had another best friend, Karen Brewer. But Karen was only in first grade, so that was no good. Nancy would have to face second grade and Ms. Colman all by herself.

Ricky Torres crawled under his bed. Then he crawled out. "I can't find them!" he shouted. "They are not anywhere!"

"How could you lose your sneakers, Ricky? Your brand-new shoes." His mother sighed. "We just bought them yesterday."

"If I cannot find my shoes, do I still have to go to school?" asked Ricky. He looked down at his bare feet.

"You certainly do," replied Mrs. Torres. "You can wear those nice brown oxfords Grandpa sent you."

Ricky found his sneakers in a hurry.

"I hope Ms. Colman is going to be nice," said Sara Ford. She was sitting at the kitchen table with her mother, her father, and her big brother Marcus. "I hope Stoneybrook Academy is going to be nice."

Sara and her family had moved to Stoneybrook, Connecticut, over the summer. Sara was still deciding whether she liked it.

"But you met Ms. Colman last week," said Marcus. "Didn't you?"

"Yes," said Sara.

"And you liked her, didn't you?"

"Yes."

"Well?"

"Well, Mommy and Daddy were right there with me. Ms. Colman was not going to be mean in front of parents. I will just have to wait and see."

Natalie Springer bent over. She pulled up her socks. She hummed a tune.

"Ready for school, honey?" called her mother.

4

Natalie looked at herself in the mirror. Her hair was falling in her face. Her glasses were slipping down her nose. Her blouse was half untucked. One shoe was untied. And her socks were already falling down again. "Ready!" Natalie called back.

"Are you nervous?" asked Mrs. Springer.

Natalie shook her head. "Nope. I liked kindergarten. I liked first grade. I love Stoneybrook Academy. I think second grade is going to be fun. I bet Ms. Colman will be fun, too."

"Nancy, hurry," said Mr. Dawes. "Karen is waiting."

"Don't forget your sweater," said Mrs. Dawes.

"Here is your lunch," said Mr. Dawes.

"And your new pencil case," said Mrs. Dawes.

"Do I really have to go to second grade?" asked Nancy.

STONEYBROOK ACADEMY

"I just love school," said Karen Brewer. "I cannot wait for first grade. Of course, I already know how to read."

"Yup," said Nancy. She was not really listening to Karen. She was playing with her seatbelt, and watching the streets fly by outside the car. And she was thinking. She was thinking about second grade and Ms. Colman and friends and meanie-mo Martha. Her stomach did not feel very good.

"Mommy?" said Karen. "Could you drive faster, please? I am in a big hurry to get to first grade."

Yick, thought Nancy.

✏ ✏ ✏

Bobby Gianelli was sitting in the back-seat of his father's car. Next to him was his little sister Alicia. Alicia was not even four yet, so she had to sit in a carseat.

"Baby, baby, baby," sang Bobby softly. He hoped his father could not hear him. "Little bitty baby." He poked Alicia's leg.

Alicia stared at Bobby. Then she poked him back.

"Daddy! Alicia touched me!" cried Bobby.

"Alicia, are you bothering your broth-er?" asked Mr. Gianelli.

Alicia looked at her father in the rear-view mirror. "No," she said.

Bobby stuck his tongue out at his sis-ter. Then he decided to have a fight with someone on the playground first thing that day. Maybe Ian Johnson. Or Chris Lamar.

Omar Harris was hopping down the sidewalk. His pack bumped against his back with every hop. Hop, hop, hop.

Bump, bump, bump. Omar had a big and very important job that day. He was walking his brother Ebon to school. Ebon was going to be in first grade. And Omar was in charge of him. It was the first time Omar and Ebon had walked to Stoneybrook Academy all by themselves. With no grown-ups.

"Remember, Ebon. I will be in Ms. Colman's room if you need anything today. Just tell your teacher to come get me," said Omar.

Ebon nodded his head. "Okay."

"And one more thing," Omar went on.

"What?"

"Remember that school is fun."

"Oh. Okay!" said Ebon.

"Nancy, you know what you need?" asked Karen Brewer.

"No," said Nancy. The car was slowing down. Nancy could see Stoneybrook Academy now.

"You need a new second-grade best

9

friend. Since Martha will not be in your class."

"I guess," replied Nancy.

"Well, I have an idea. My *other* best friend is Hannie Papadakis. And Hannie is going to be in Ms. Colman's room with you. She should be *your* best friend, too. Then you would have a second-grade best friend again."

"Okay," said Nancy. "Maybe." She paused. "Oh, no!" she cried. "Look! There is Bobby Gianelli. Bully Bobby. He is always fighting with people. He scares me."

Karen looked at Bobby. He did seem scary. He was running after another boy and yelling at him. Karen leaned out of the car window. She shouted, "Hey, Bully Bobby! Quit picking on everyone! Go to your room where you belong!"

The bell rang then, and the kids on the playground hurried inside. Nancy and Karen hurried after them.

Second grade had begun.

3

MS. COLMAN

"**W**ell, here is my classroom," said Karen. She and Nancy were standing by the door to one of the first-grade rooms. "See you later."

" 'Bye, Karen," said Nancy sadly.

Nancy looked down the hallway. She knew where her room was. She walked toward it very slowly. Natalie ran by her. Omar ran by her. Ricky ran by her.

"Hey, slowpoke!" Ricky called to Nancy.

Nancy stopped outside Ms. Colman's room. She poked her head in the door.

"BOO!" shouted Bully Bobby.

"Aughh!" shrieked Nancy.

"Scared you, you baby," said Bobby. He glared at Nancy.

"Leave me alone."

"Not unless you tell your little first-grade friend to leave *me* alone," replied Bobby. Then he ran after Sara. "Hey, you! New kid!"

"Oh, make like a bee and buzz off," said Sara. Then she ignored Bobby.

Nancy took another step into the room. She saw Natalie, Ricky, the Barkan twins, and some other kids she knew from kindergarten and first grade. And she saw a lot of kids she did not know.

"Good morning, boys and girls," said a grown-up's voice.

Standing in the doorway behind Nancy was Ms. Colman. She was smiling. She was smiling even though Ian Johnson was pretending to brush his hair with an eraser. And even though Audrey Green was giving herself a tattoo with a red

Magic Marker. And even though Hank Reubens was tickling Leslie Morris and had made Leslie fall on the floor.

Ms. Colman stepped over to her desk. She set a pile of papers on it. The kids in her class ran to find desks of their own. When they were seated, all the boys were in the back and all the girls were in the front. "Hmm," said Ms. Colman. "This will not do."

Ms. Colman told each of her students where to sit. When they had switched places, Nancy found herself in the back row. At the end of the row was that pest Ricky Torres. Next to him was Hannie Papadakis, Karen's friend. Nancy sat on the other side of Hannie. And next to Nancy, at the other end of the row, was . . . nobody.

That was probably supposed to have been Martha's desk, thought Nancy. I would have been sitting next to my best friend.

Nancy looked at Hannie. She was about to lean over and whisper, "Psst! Hey! Hannie Papadakis!"

But Hannie was busy whispering to Sara Ford who sat in front of her. Then Terri Barkan turned around and asked Hannie if she could borrow a pencil. And then Ricky passed a note to Hannie.

Nancy sighed. She gazed around the room. Who would be her second-grade best friend?

"Girls and boys," said Ms. Colman, "before we begin today, I would like you to put your things away in your cubbies. The cubbies are over there." Ms. Colman pointed. "I have written your names on them. Will the students in the front row please find their cubbies?"

Row by row, the kids in Ms. Colman's class put away their lunch boxes and book-bags and backpacks and extra sneakers. They hung up their sweaters and jackets and baseball caps. Chris Lamar put away his rubber football. Tammy Barkan put away her walking robot action figure.

When everyone was finished, Ms. Colman said, "Okay, girls and boys. Listen up."

4

THE PEST

"It is time for roll," said Ms. Colman. "I will call you in alphabetical order by your last names. A names first, B names next, and so on. When I call your name, please raise your hand and say, 'Here.'" Ms. Colman's attendance book was open. She was holding a pencil. "Tammy Barkan," she called.

"Here!" One of the twins raised her hand.

"Terri Barkan."

"Here!" The other twin raised her hand.

"Nancy Dawes."

"Here," said Nancy softly.

Ms. Colman made a check in her book each time someone said, "Here." She had made three checks so far.

"Sara Ford, Bobby Gianelli, Jannie Gilbert." Check, check, check. "Audrey Green, Omar Harris, Ian Johnson, Chris Lamar, Leslie Morris." Five more checks. "Hannie Papadakis, Hank Reubens, Natalie Springer, Ricky Torres." Check, check, check, check. Fifteen checks in all.

Ms. Colman put her book down. "Good. Everyone is here today. Now boys and girls, please raise your hand if you brought a pencil to school." Nine kids raised their hands. "That is fine," said Ms. Colman. She handed out fat blue pencils to the kids who had not brought any. "I keep spare pencils in my desk," she went on. "And paper will be kept on the shelf by the pencil sharpener."

Ms. Colman had a lot of first-day-of-school things to do. She reminded her students where the nurse's office was. She reminded them where the bathrooms and

the cafeteria were. Then she began to hand out workbooks and reading books and math books and science books.

Ricky poked Hannie with an eraser.

"Pest," said Hannie. She edged closer to Nancy.

Nancy looked around the room. Who would be her new best friend? Maybe Leslie. No. Leslie was whispering to Jannie. They were already best friends.

"Excuse me, Ms. Colman?" said Natalie. "I lost my pencil." Natalie pulled up her socks as she searched under her desk. Finally Ms. Colman gave her a new pencil.

Bully Bobby leaned over to Chris and whispered, "I am going to get you on the playground today."

Hannie took the reading book Sara Ford passed back to her. Then she whispered, "Hey, I like your barrettes. I have a barrette collection. My best barrettes are shaped like a hamburger and French fries."

Nancy decided Hannie was a chatter-box.

Ricky must have thought so, too. He poked her again.

"Quit it, pest!" Hannie whispered loudly.

"Ahem," said Ms. Colman from the front of the room. (But she was smiling.) "May I have your attention, please? I want to tell you about our first class project this year. The project is about pets, but it is also about getting to know one another. Today, tomorrow, and Thursday we will work on three activities about pets. We will work in groups. The groups will change each day. By Friday, you will have had a chance to work with most of your classmates. And something special will happen on Friday. Friday will be Pet Day during Show and Share time. On Pet Day, you may bring a pet to school if you have one. You may show it to the class, and tell us something about it. If you do not have a live pet, you may bring in a stuffed animal."

"Hmphh," whispered Hannie. "A *stuffed* animal. What good is that? That is stupid."

"We will end our pet unit," Ms. Colman went on, "next week. We will end it with a field trip to the pet store. At the store, we will buy a pet for our classroom. The Parent-Teacher-Student Organization has raised enough money so that each class may get a pet."

The kids in Ms. Colman's class looked at each other and grinned. Even Bobby said, "Cool!"

"What kind of pet will we get?" asked Ian.

"That is what our pet activities will help us decide," replied Ms. Colman. "We will work on our first pet activity after recess today. Right now, it is time for reading."

5

THE PETASAURUS

When Ms. Colman's kids returned to their class after recess they found a surprise. Their desks had been pushed into three groups, with five desks in each group.

"Good afternoon, girls and boys," said Ms. Colman. "Are you ready to start thinking about pets?"

"Yes!" said her students.

"Terrific. Then I will divide you into your groups. In the first group will be Tammy Barkan, Sara Ford, Ian Johnson, Nancy Dawes, and Leslie Morris. You may sit here." Ms. Colman pointed to the desks by the windows.

Nancy walked to the desks. She sat down at one. Her back was turned toward Ms. Colman, but she could hear her teacher calling out the names of the kids in the other two groups. She looked around at Tammy, Sara, Ian, and Leslie. Who could be her second-grade best friend? Not Ian. He was a boy. Tammy? Maybe. But Nancy thought Tammy's best friend was probably her twin, Terri. Sara? Maybe. But she was the new girl. Nancy did not know a thing about her. That left Leslie. Leslie already had a best friend, Jannie. But at least Jannie was not her twin sister. Maybe Leslie could have two best friends like Karen Brewer did. Nancy sort of remembered Leslie from kindergarten, and she thought Leslie seemed okay. A little bossy, but okay.

"Class," Ms. Colman said loudly.

Nancy turned around in her seat. She smiled at Leslie as she did so. But Leslie was waving across the room to Jannie.

"Today," said Ms. Colman, "we are

going to talk about what makes the ideal pet. That means the best pet or the perfect pet. I want you to make a list of those things together. I will walk around the room and help you. Then I want you to use this list to invent an imaginary perfect pet, and name it. Later, you can choose one person in your group to tell the other groups about your pet." Ms. Colman handed each group a large piece of paper and a red crayon. "Okay. Go to work," she said.

Nancy looked at the crayon in front of her. "Who should do the writing?" she asked her group.

"I will," said Leslie. "I am sure I have the best handwriting." Leslie grabbed the crayon. "All right. What makes a good pet?"

"It is easy to take care of," replied Ian.

"It eats neatly," said Tammy.

"It keeps you company," said Sara.

"How do you spell 'company'?" asked Leslie.

"We better ask for help," said Nancy. She turned to look for Ms. Colman. "Mommy!" she called.

"Mommy!" Leslie repeated. "Hey, you called Ms. Colman Mommy!" Leslie began to laugh. She could not stop.

Nancy's face turned red. She hoped Ms. Colman had not heard her. She did not think she had. Ms. Colman was busy with another group.

"You called her Mommy!" Leslie said again. "Hee hee hee hee hee."

Nancy glared at Leslie. Leslie certainly was not going to be her new best friend. She was way too mean.

After Leslie stopped laughing, Nancy tried to think about the perfect pet. With Ms. Colman's help, her group made a long, long list. They wrote down things about how their pet should act, how it should look, and tricks it could do.

They named their perfect pet the Petasaurus.

By the end of the day, Nancy felt a little better — until she heard Leslie whisper to Jannie, "You know what Nancy Dawes did? She called Ms. Colman Mommy!"

Jannie turned to look at Nancy. She and Leslie were both laughing.

I knew second grade would be horrible, thought Nancy.

6

BARF AND ME

Wednesday was the second day of school. After recess, Ms. Colman said to her students, "Class, it is time for our next pet project. Today you will work in three different groups. And each group will write a story together, a story about a pet."

Omar raised his hand. "A true story?" he asked.

"If you like," replied Ms. Colman. "Or it could be a made-up story."

"Does it have to be about a real animal?" asked Hannie.

"Can the pet talk?" asked Terri.

"Those things are up to you," said Ms.

Colman. "I want you to think about pets, to write a story, and to work together. All right. In group one is . . ."

Nancy found herself in a brand-new group. She would be writing the story with Natalie, Bully Bobby, Omar, and Chris. Yuck. This was not a good group. Too many boys. And one of them was *Bobby*. Nancy moved as far away from him as she could. The only person in this group who might be her new best friend was Natalie Springer.

"Who is going to write down our story?" asked Natalie.

"You or Nancy," said Bobby. "Girls always have the best handwriting."

"Well, let's see about that," replied Natalie. "Everybody — write your name on this paper."

The kids wrote their names on the large sheet of paper Ms. Colman had given them. They wrote very, very carefully.

"Ha! Omar has the best writing!" exclaimed Natalie.

So Omar picked up a pencil. "Okay. How do we start?"

"Let's write a story," began Natalie, "about a girl and her dog. And the dog is named Barf."

"Barf!" shrieked Omar.

"You mean Bart," said Nancy.

"No, *Barf*," Natalie repeated.

"But Barf — " Nancy began to say.

No one heard her, though. The boys were laughing too loudly.

Natalie bent over. She pulled up her droopy socks. She tried to tuck in her shirt. Nancy noticed a bit of carrot on one of Natalie's front teeth.

"I *want* to *write* a *story* about a *dog* named *Barf*," said Natalie slowly.

"Okay, okay," said Chris.

The kids settled down. They wrote a story about a dog named Barf. They finished before the other groups did.

Bobby made an announcement to his group. "I," he said, "am bringing my dog to school on Pet Day. My parents said I could."

"Cool," replied Chris. "I am going to bring our rabbit."

"You have a rabbit?" Natalie asked Chris.

Nancy slumped down in her chair. She did not have a pet. What was she going to do on Pet Day? She had a beautiful stuffed monkey. But Hannie had said bringing in a stuffed animal was stupid.

"Class," said Ms. Colman from the front of the room. "You have worked hard on your stories today. Now it is time to share them with the other groups. Let me see. Nancy, would you please read your group's story aloud?"

"Me?" replied Nancy. She did not want to read a story about a dog named Barf. But Ms. Colman was the teacher, and she had asked her to read it. Slowly Nancy stood up. "Well," she began, "our story is about a dog. And *Natalie Springer* said he should be named, um, Barf."

The kids laughed. Nancy glared at Natalie. No way was Natalie going to be her second-grade best friend. Then she read the story. She read it fast and sat down quickly. Some of the kids were still laughing. But they were looking at Natalie, not at Nancy. Nancy did not feel so bad.

Except about the pet. She did wish she had a real, live pet to bring to school on Pet Day.

GERBIL, HAMSTER, RAT

"Group time again!" called Ms. Colman. She clapped her hands twice.

It was Thursday afternoon. Recess was over. The kids in Ms. Colman's class had returned to their room. And once again they found their desks pushed into three groups.

"When I call your names, please form your new groups," said Ms. Colman. "Then I will tell you about today's assignment."

Nancy sat at a group of desks by the classroom door. In her group were Hank Reubens, Jannie Gilbert, Hannie Papadakis, and Terri Barkan. Could one of *them* be her new best friend? Nancy decided she was tired of looking for a new best friend. She sat back and waited for her teacher to talk about the next assignment.

"Today," said Ms. Colman, "we will start deciding on the pet we will get next week. You have already been thinking about pets. And you have written down some things that would make an ideal pet. Now I want you to think about what animal would make the best classroom pet. Talk about this in your groups. Then I would like each group to choose the pet they want to buy next week. When the three pets have been chosen, we will vote on one. And that is the pet we will get. Any questions?"

Jannie raised her hand. "Can we really choose any pet?"

"Yes," replied Ms. Colman. "As long as it would be a good classroom pet. Would a dog be a good classroom pet?"

"No!" cried Ricky.

"Why not?" asked Ms. Colman.

"Because you cannot leave it alone at night."

"That's right. So think carefully. Okay, boys and girls. Time to get to work."

Hannie and Hank and Nancy and Terri and Jannie looked at one another.

"Well," said Terri, "what kind of pet should we get?"

"I want a cat," said Jannie.

"A cat!" exclaimed Hank. "We cannot get a cat. A cat would not be happy living in a classroom. It would want to go outside. And it would not want to be alone at night."

"How about a monkey?" asked Jannie.

"Now that is just silly," said Hannie. "We have to get a smaller pet that can live in a cage."

"A gerbil," said Terri.

"A hamster," said Hank.

"What kind of pet do you want?" Hannie asked Nancy.

Nancy shrugged.

"We could get fish," suggested Jannie.

"Or a rat," said Hannie.

"A rat would be easy to take care of," said Hank.

"And fun to watch," said Terri.

"Do you like rats?" Hannie asked Nancy.

"Yup." Nancy nodded. And smiled.

Hannie smiled back. "Okay. Our group chooses a rat," she said.

The other groups had not made decisions yet.

Hank said, "Guess what I am bringing in for Pet Day tomorrow. My dog, Jack," he went on, before anyone could guess. "I have a canary named Sassy, too. But I am only going to bring one pet to school."

"I am bringing in my cat. Her name is Eloise," said Jannie.

"I am bringing in a surprise," said Terri.

"I am bringing in Noodle, our poodle," said Hannie.

"What are you bringing, Nancy?" asked Terri.

"I do not know yet," Nancy replied. "Maybe . . . well, I do not know."

Hannie leaned over to Nancy. "Do you have a pet?" she whispered.

"No," Nancy admitted.

"That's okay," said Hannie.

Nancy smiled at Hannie again. She decided Hannie was nice.

8

A BIG PROBLEM

"It is time," said Ms. Colman, "to choose our class pet. Girls and boys, please put your desks back in their rows."

The kids in Ms. Colman's class bustled around the room. When their desks were in order, they sat in four neat rows, with four desks in each row, the empty desk in the back.

"Thank you," said Ms. Colman. "All right, these are the pets you have chosen. Group one chose a hamster." (Ms. Colman wrote *hamster* on the blackboard.) "Group two chose a rat." (Ms. Colman wrote *rat*.) "And group three chose a rabbit." (She added *rabbit* to the list.) "These are very good choices. Any of these animals would make a fine pet for our classroom. Now we need to decide which one we will get. We will do this by voting. I would like each of you to vote for two animals. Please raise your hand when I call out the animals. Remember, you must vote for *two* of them."

In the back of the room, Nancy sat eagerly at her desk. When Ms. Colman said, "Hamster," she held very still. When she said, "Rat," she raised her hand high. When Ms. Colman said, "Rabbit," Nancy raised her hand again.

Ms. Colman counted the votes. "Ten for the hamster, seven for the rat, thirteen for the rabbit," she said. "Okay, we will take the rat off the list."

"Boo," muttered Hank.

"Now you will vote for either the hamster or the rabbit," Ms. Colman went on. "Just one vote this time. Hamster?"

Seven hands shot up.

"Rabbit?"

Eight hands shot up.

Ms. Colman smiled. "The rabbit wins!" she announced. "Next week we will go to the pet store and choose a rabbit."

Eight kids cried, "Yea!"

Seven kids were silent.

Finally Natalie raised her hand. "But I do not want a rabbit," she said. "I want a hamster."

"Me, too," said six other voices.

Ms. Colman sat patiently at her desk. "We took a vote," she reminded her class. "You voted for the rabbit."

"*I* didn't," said Ricky.

"Neither did I," said Natalie and Terri and Omar and Chris and Leslie and Audrey. They crossed their arms. And Audrey added, "Seven people is almost half the class."

"Hmm. That's true," said Ms. Colman. "Almost half the class does not want to get a rabbit. What do you think we should do?"

"Get a hamster!" called out Bobby.

Ms. Colman smiled. "I am afraid that is not the answer. We have a big problem. Let me think about this."

Just before the bell rang at the end of the day, Ms. Colman said, "Class, I still am not sure what to do about our pet. For now, I think we better call off our field trip to the pet store. We just cannot get a rabbit if half the class will be so unhappy. I promise we will get a pet. But I must think about the best way to do it."

Nancy glanced at Hannie. She smiled at her. Hannie smiled back. So far, Ms. Colman was the fairest teacher they had ever had.

In the front of the room, Ms. Colman smiled, too. "Tomorrow is Pet Day!" she reminded her students.

9

PET DAY

"Ms. Colman must be the best teacher in the world," said Ebon Harris to his big brother Omar. "She said you can bring *Buster* to *school*?"

"Yup," said Omar. He gave Buster one last brushing. Buster was the Harrises' sheepdog, and Omar was very proud of him.

"Why?" asked Ebon.

"Why what?" replied Omar.

"Why did she say you could bring Buster to school?"

"Because today is Pet Day."

"Is he all ready?" Tammy asked Terri.

Terri peered inside the box she was holding. The lid of the box said *Happy Feet Shoes*. The twins had punched holes in it with their hole puncher. "All ready," replied Terri. "Ready for his first day of school." She giggled.

"Do you think we should dress him up or something?" asked Tammy.

"Nah. He never lets us. . . . Come on. Let's tell Daddy we are ready for him to drive us and Frank to school."

"Won't the kids be surprised when they meet Frank?" added Tammy.

"Okay, you guys, I hope you like school," said Hannie. She was sitting in the backseat of her mother's car. Next to her was her little sister. In the front were her mother and Linny, her brother. In her lap were Noodle the Poodle and Myrtle the Turtle.

"Are you sure you are allowed to bring two pets to school?" asked Linny.

"Yes," replied Hannie. "I have a special plan."

Nancy walked into her classroom feeling nervous. It was Pet Day. And she had not brought a pet. Not even her stuffed monkey. She looked around the room. She saw Omar with a beautiful woolly dog. She saw Terri and Tammy with a shoebox. She saw cats and cages and two more dogs. Then she saw Natalie. Natalie was sitting at her desk with no pet. She saw Ian. Ian

was sitting at his desk with no pet. She saw Sara. On Sara's desk was an old stuffed chipmunk. Nancy began to feel better.

"Hey, Tammy, Terri. What do you guys have in the box?" asked Jannie. Jannie's cat Eloise was wandering around the room. She was hissing. Jannie's dad was standing in the back of the room with some other parents. Some grandparents, too. Mr. Gilbert was keeping a close watch on Eloise.

Terri and Tammy grinned. They opened the box.

"Meet Frank," said Tammy.

"Ribbit," said Frank.

"Ew, a *frog*!" screeched Sara.

"We better keep Frank away from Eloise," said Terri.

"Nancy! Hey, Nancy Dawes!" called a voice.

Nancy turned around. Standing in the doorway was Hannie. Behind her was her mother. Mrs. Papadakis was carrying Sari, and leading Noodle the Poodle on his leash. Hannie was carrying her turtle. She held her out to Nancy. "Here," said Hannie. "This is Myrtle the Turtle. You can borrow her today."

"I *can*?" replied Nancy. "You mean, I will have my own pet?"

"Just for Pet Day," said Hannie quickly.

"Boy . . . thanks!" cried Nancy.

10

BEST FRIENDS

"Welcome, mothers and fathers and grandparents and pets," said Ms. Colman. "Welcome to Pet Day."

The morning had begun. Ms. Colman was standing in front of the blackboard. Her students were seated at their desks. The mothers and fathers were standing in the back of the room. And everywhere — on leashes, in carriers, in boxes, and on desks — were dogs and cats and frogs and turtles and stuffed animals.

"This morning," Ms. Colman said to her students, "anyone who brought in a pet may come to the front of the room and tell us a little bit about it. Who would like to begin?"

"Me! Me!" called Hank.

Hank's father handed him a leash. At the end of the leash was a friendly black dog.

"This is my dog, Jack," said Hank proudly. "He is a mutt. We got him from the pound. He is — Hey, stop that, Jack! No biting!"

"Yeah, no biting *me*," said Natalie. She pulled her legs under her desk.

"He is two years old," Hank went on. "Jack's favorite — No biting! His favorite toy is — No *biting*, Jack! Is an old — I said, no biting! And no chasing ca — "

"Daddy! Save Eloise!" cried Jannie.

Jack chased Eloise twice around the room. Finally Mr. Gilbert put Eloise back in her carrier. Eloise hissed loudly. Mr. Reubens led Jack into the hall for a walk.

"I wanted to go next," Jannie announced. "But I will have to let Eloise calm

Science 10:00 - 11:00 am

down first. She is all upset now."

Nancy raised her hand. "Could I go next?" she asked, and Ms. Colman nodded. Nancy carried Myrtle to the front of the room. "This is Myrtle the Turtle," she began. "Myrtle is, um, she is . . . hmm. I forget how old Myrtle is." In the back of the room, Hannie held up one finger. "Oh, yeah. She is a year old," said Nancy. "She is very, um, friendly. And . . . and . . . let me see. Her shell is quite hard. She is — "

"What kind of turtle is she, Nancy?" asked Ian.

"Well, everyone knows she is a box turtle," spoke up Hannie.

"She likes to play, and she is a very good pet," Nancy finished up. Then she sat down in a hurry. There. Done. She had not even had to admit that Myrtle was not her own pet. (Although she thought the kids knew anyway.) "Thanks, Hannie," whispered Nancy. "You are a great friend."

"You're welcome," Hannie whispered back. "You are a great friend, too."

"I am?"

"Sure. Karen has told me about you. You *sound* like a good friend, anyway."

In the front of the room, Chris was talking about his rabbit. But Nancy and Hannie were not listening.

"Is Hannie your real name or a nick-name?" Nancy wanted to know.

"Nickname. It is short for Hannah."

"Do you have a best friend here? In our room?" asked Nancy.

Hannie shook her head. "Karen is my only best friend."

"Mine, too," said Hannie.

"Girls! Shhh!" said Ms. Colman. "Please pay attention to Chris."

Nancy and Hannie quieted down until Chris finished. Then Nancy leaned over to Hannie and whispered, "Do you want to be my second-grade best friend?"

"Sure," replied Hannie. "And you can be mine."

Nancy Dawes had a second-grade best friend at last.

KAREN'S SURPRISE

"Ing," said Nancy Dawes to herself. "Ing, ing, ing."

It was Monday morning, and Nancy was bent over a worksheet. She was adding *ing* to words. Some words were easy, such as *start*. She just added *ing* after the last letter. But some words were tricky. She had to remember, for instance, to add another *t* at the end of *pat* before she put on the *ing*.

"P-a-t-t-i-n-g," Nancy was whispering, when the door to Ms. Colman's room opened. Nancy glanced up.

Karen Brewer walked through the door. A teacher's aide was with her.

"Good morning, Mr. Abrams. Good

morning, Karen," said Ms. Colman. Ms. Colman was smiling. "Karen, this will be your cubby."

Her cubby? That was when Nancy noticed that Karen was carrying her jacket, her extra sneakers, and everything she had brought to school that morning. Nancy could not believe it. Was Karen going to be in her class?

Mr. Abrams left the room. Karen put away her things.

Then Ms. Colman said, "Class, this is Karen Brewer. She started out in first grade last week, but we have decided to move her to second grade."

"Smarty pants," whispered Ricky.

"So she is joining our class. Karen, you may take that empty seat next to Nancy Dawes in the back of the room."

Karen grinned at Nancy and Hannie. Then she headed for the last row of desks. As she passed Bobby's desk, he whispered, "First-grade baby." He stuck his foot into the aisle.

Karen stepped over the foot. She whispered back, "You leave me alone, you big bully. You do not scare me." Then she hurried to the back of the room and sat down next to Nancy.

"Karen!" Nancy said. She tried to whisper, but she was too excited. "Did you know you were going to be in my class?"

"Mommy told me yesterday, but I wanted to surprise you. Isn't this a good surprise? I can — "

"Girls," said Ms. Colman. "Quiet, please."

Karen sat quietly at her desk. This was very difficult for her. She wanted to say a million things. She wanted to say that she was best friends with Nancy and also with Hannie. She wanted to say that it was so great that Nancy and Hannie were best friends now, too. She wanted to say that this meant they could all be best friends together. Plus, she wanted to say that that very morning she had watched a cartoon about a great big chicken and a little tiny chicken hawk —

"Class," said Ms. Colman, "I have not forgotten about our problem."

Karen raised her hand. "What problem?"

Ms. Colman explained to Karen about the hamster and the rabbit and the vote. "So I would like you to vote one more time," she said. "In case any of you have changed your minds."

Karen raised her hand again. "You are voting for a hamster or a rabbit?" she asked, just to make sure. "Why not a guinea pig? Guinea pigs are great pets. I played with one once. He was very, very friendly."

"Hey, a guinea pig," said Sara. "That *would* be a good pet."

"I like guinea pigs," said Hank.

"Me too," said Audrey.

"Hmm. Well, let's add a guinea pig to the list and take another vote," said Ms. Colman. "How many of you want to get a guinea pig?"

Sixteen hands shot into the air.

"Every single one of you!" exclaimed Ms. Colman. "It is unanimous then. Okay, our field trip is on. I will give you permission slips this afternoon. Please ask your parents to sign them. Remember to bring them back to me tomorrow. We will go to the pet store on Wednesday."

THE PERFECT PET

On Tuesday, the kids in Ms. Colman's class were very busy.

"Tomorrow," said Ms. Colman, "when we go to the pet store, we must know exactly what we need to buy. We will need quite a few things besides the guinea pig. Can you think of some of those things?"

"Food!" called out Tammy.

"Right," said Ms. Colman. "What kind of food?" (The kids looked at each other. They did not raise their hands.) "We need to find out what guinea pigs eat, then," Ms. Colman went on. "What else should we buy?"

"A cage," said Audrey.

"Good. How big?" asked Ms. Colman.

The kids did not know. So Ms. Colman took her class to the library. The librarian helped them find books about pets and guinea pigs. They read about what guinea pigs eat. They read about how much exercise they need. They read about how guinea pigs play and sleep and feed their babies, and about how to keep them healthy.

Ms. Colman helped the kids make a

list of things to buy at the pet store the next day. At the end of the list they wrote: "One guinea pig, the perfect pet! (Brown with white spots, maybe.)"

In the afternoon, Ms. Colman said to the class, "I want to talk to you about our trip tomorrow. We will go to the pet store in a yellow school bus. When you are on the bus, you must stay in your seats. No standing up or running around. And you must stay with your partners."

"What partners?" asked Ian.

"I am going to assign partners in a few minutes," said Ms. Colman. "You must stay with your partners on the way to the bus, on the bus, in the store, and all the way home," said Ms. Colman.

Leslie wrinkled her nose. "Do we have to hold hands?" she asked.

"Not on the bus or in the store," replied Ms. Colman. "But the rest of the time you must hold hands. All right. Here are the partners for tomorrow: Hank and

Ricky, Audrey and Sara, Karen and Nancy . . ."

"Yea! We get to be partners!" Karen whispered to Nancy.

"What about Hannie?" Nancy whispered back.

Hannie's partner was Tammy. That was okay with Hannie.

"See you tomorrow!" called Ms. Colman as the bell rang.

13

THE SCHOOL BUS

"Two by two!" Ms. Colman reminded her students. "Hold hands until you are seated on the bus."

The kids in Ms. Colman's class were ready for their trip. They were lined up by the door to their room in two short lines, holding hands with their partners. Ms. Colman stood at the front of the lines. She was holding the list of things to buy at the pet store. At the back of the lines stood Omar's father. Mr. Harris was the room parent for the trip.

"Remember the bus rules," said Ms. Colman as she opened the door and led her students into the hall.

63

"Oh, goody, goody, goody. I am so excited!" said Natalie to Terri.

"We are going to get a *pet*!" Karen exclaimed to Nancy.

"Your hand is sweaty," said Bobby to Ian.

"I love buses," said Hank to Ricky.

Just as Ms. Colman had promised, a big yellow school bus was waiting in the parking lot outside of Stoneybrook Academy. The kids climbed onto it and scrambled for seats.

Bobby and Ian claimed the very last seat in the back of the bus. "So we can bounce over bumps," said Bobby.

Karen and Nancy both wanted to sit by the window.

"You *can't* both sit there," Hannie said.

"We can if Nancy sits in my lap," replied Karen.

Ms. Colman would not allow that, so they decided to take turns.

Soon the driver closed the door at the front of the bus. Then she turned the bus slowly into the street.

"Let's sing!" cried Terri.

"Yeah!" said Omar. " 'A Hundred Bottles of Pop on the Wall'!"

"No, 'The Wheels on the Bus,' " said Audrey.

So the boys sang one song while the girls sang another.

Mr. Harris put his hands over his ears. "Help! I am getting a headache."

"So am I," said the bus driver.

The kids quieted down.

"Here we are," said Ms. Colman a few minutes later.

The kids looked out the windows. The bus had pulled up in front of Noah's Ark, the pet store, in downtown Stoneybrook. The owner of Noah's Ark was standing outside. He waved to the kids.

"Okay, two by two," said Ms. Colman. And her students filed off the bus and into the store to buy the perfect pet.

THE PET STORE

"Good morning, boys and girls. My name is Tom Hanley. This is my pet store. I am going to give you a hand today. I understand you would like to buy a guinea pig."

Sara raised her hand. "And guinea pig food," she added.

"And everything else a guinea pig needs," said Chris.

The kids in Ms. Colman's class were seated on the floor at the back of the pet store. They were in the fish section. Along the walls around them were aquariums full of brightly colored fish. And standing before them was Mr. Hanley.

"Do you know everything there is to know about pets?" Hannie asked Mr. Hanley.

Mr. Hanley smiled. "I do not know *every*thing," he said. "But I know quite a bit. Enough to help you out. Are there any more questions?"

Bobby raised his hand. "Can we choose the guinea pig now?"

Mr. Hanley looked at Ms. Colman. Ms. Colman said, "Let's pick out the guinea pig's supplies first. We will choose our pet last. Now Mr. Hanley, we are working with a budget," Ms. Colman continued. "We have only a certain amount of money to spend. We want a nice cage and good supplies, but nothing too fancy."

Mr. Hanley folded his arms. "Hmm," he said. "Let me think. All right. We will look at cages first. Right this way, please."

Ms. Colman's students followed Mr. Hanley to the front of the store. Together they decided on a cage. It was big enough for a guinea pig, but not too expensive. Mr. Hanley set the cage on the counter by the cash register.

"Food next," said Karen. She was hopping up and down with excitement.

Mr. Hanley helped the kids choose food and dishes and toys and more. He stacked each item on the counter next to the cage.

"And now for the most important thing," said Ms. Colman finally. "Our guinea pig." She smiled at her class.

"We would like a brown one with white spots, please," said Jannie.

"Brown with white spots," repeated Mr. Hanley. "Let's see what we can do. Our guinea pigs are over here, in these three cages."

Ms. Colman's students rushed to peer into the cages.

"Oh, look! How cute!" cried Leslie.

"Hey, those two are playing!" said Omar.

"That one is sleeping," said Audrey.

"There is a brown and white one!" exclaimed Terri.

"Silly, it has no spots," said Tammy.

"I like that black and white one better," said Nancy.

"That one has no spots either," said Tammy.

The kids stood in front of the cages for a long, long time.

They argued. "Why does it have to be brown and white?" asked Ricky.

They laughed. "That one is the funni-est!" said Ian.

They discussed things. "Spots are nice, but why do we care what it looks like?" said Sara. "We just want a nice, friendly pet."

They decided which guinea pigs they did *not* want. At last, only two were left. Both were brown and white. Both liked to play. Both seemed nice and friendly. But only one of them sat in their hands and whistled happily.

"I think he likes you," said Mr. Hanley.

"Shall we take him?" Ms. Colman asked her students.

"Yes!" they cried.

Hootie

Mr. Hanley put the guinea pig into a special box for the trip to his new home. The kids in Ms. Colman's class carried his cage and toys and supplies onto the bus. Then they found seats with their partners.

"Can I hold the guinea pig, Ms. Colman?" Hank called out.

"No, I want to!" cried Natalie.

Everyone wanted to hold the guinea pig. Mr. Harris held him instead.

"You will have your turns when we are back in our classroom," Ms. Colman told the kids.

The school bus rattled toward Stoneybrook Academy. The girls sang "I've Been

Working on the Railroad." The boys sang "This Old Man." Then they all sang "The Ants Go Marching." When the bus stopped, everyone piled out. The kids carried the pet supplies to their classroom. Mr. Harris carried the guinea pig.

When Mr. Harris had put the guinea pig on Ms. Colman's desk, he said, "I must go to my office now. But I enjoyed our trip to the pet store. Good-bye, kids. Good-bye, Ms. Colman. Good-bye, Omar." Then he left.

"Let's show the guinea pig his new home!" said Leslie.

"No, let's set up his cage," said Ian.

Half the kids showed the guinea pig around the room, while the other half set to work on his cage.

"See? Here are the cubbies," Karen said to the guinea pig.

Sniff, sniff, sniff went the guinea pig's nose.

"Here is the reading corner," said Hank.

"This is *my* desk," said Natalie proudly.

"And this is Ms. Colman's," added Jannie.

The other kids were busy with the cage. They spread shavings in it. They set out food and water. They arranged the toys. At last it was ready for the guinea pig. Ms. Colman set him gently in the cage. He walked around slowly. *Sniff, sniff, sniff* went his nose. Then he let out his whistle.

"He likes it," said Ricky.

"Well, there is just one thing left to do," said Ms. Colman. Her students looked at her. "One important thing. The guinea pig still needs . . ."

"A name!" cried Audrey.

"Exactly," said Ms. Colman.

"Bradford," said Chris. "That is what we should name him."

"Bradford?" exclaimed Jannie. "Tsk. Silly. How about Fuzzy?"

"How about Spot?" asked Ian.

"No, Wiggles," said Terri.

"Barf," said Natalie.

"Uh-oh," said Ms. Colman.

"Let's choose three names and take another vote," suggested Omar.

And that is what the kids in Ms. Colman's class did. They divided into three groups. Each group settled on one name.

"What are the names?" asked Ms. Colman.

"Fuzzy," said group one. "Because of his fur."

"Hootie," said group two. "Because of his whistle."

"Timothy," said group three. "Because we just like it."

The class voted on the names. Fourteen kids voted for Hootie.

"Hootie it is then," said Ms. Colman with a smile. "And now it is time for math. Please take out your books."

Hootie explored his cage. And Nancy sat happily at her desk, between Hannie and Karen. Her two best friends. She decided that second grade was off to a great start.

About the Author

ANN M. MARTIN lives in New York City and loves animals, especially cats. She has two cats of her own, Mouse and Rosie.

Other books by Ann M. Martin that you might enjoy are *Stage Fright*; *Me and Katie (the Pest)*; and the books in *The Baby-sitters Club* series.

Ann likes ice cream and *I Love Lucy*. And she has her own little sister, whose name is Jane.

THE KIDS IN MS. COLMAN'S CLASS

A new series by Ann M. Martin

Don't miss #2
Author Day

At the front of the room, Hank Reubens and Bobby Gianelli were drawing a picture of Natalie Springer on the chalkboard. Audrey Green was throwing an eraser at Ian Johnson. In the back of the room, Sara Ford and the twins, Tammy and Terri Barkan, were trying to play hopscotch. Chris Lamar was doodling on his sneakers with a marker.

The room was noisy. Nobody was playing with the games. A paper plane flew through the air.

Ms. Colman clapped her hands. "Boys and girls! May I have your attention, please? Class? . . . *Class!*"

The kids stopped what they were doing. They looked at their teacher.

"This is pandemonium," said Ms. Colman. "You are too loud and too wild. Please go to your seats. I think we need a story break." When the room was quiet, Ms. Colman said, "Ricky, would you please choose a book for us?"

Ricky grinned. "Sure," he said. He hurried to the reading corner behind Nancy and Karen. He knew just which book to choose. *Sloppy Sam*, by Mr. Robert Bennett. Robert Bennett was Ricky's favorite author. And *Sloppy Sam* was Ricky's favorite book by his favorite author. The kids in Ms. Colman's class had heard it dozens of times, but they would not mind hearing it again. Robert Bennett's books were so, so funny. Ricky especially liked that Mr. Bennett wrote his books *and* drew the pictures for them.

Ricky handed *Sloppy Sam* to Ms. Colman. "Here," he said.

"Goody!" said Sara. "*Sloppy Sam* again."

"Cool," said Omar Harris.

And the kids settled down to listen to one of Mr. Bennett's giggle books.

LITTLE 🍎 APPLE®

Here are some of our favorite Little Apples.

Once you take a bite out of a Little Apple book—you'll want to read more!

Books for Kids with BIG Appetites!

☐ NA45899-X **Amber Brown Is Not a Crayon**
   Paula Danziger **$2.99**

☐ NA42833-0 **Catwings** Ursula K. LeGuin **$3.50**

☐ NA42832-2 **Catwings Return** Ursula K. LeGuin **$3.50**

☐ NA41821-1 **Class Clown** Johanna Hurwitz **$3.50**

☐ NA42400-9 **Five True Horse Stories** Margaret Davidson **$3.50**

☐ NA42401-7 **Five True Dog Stories** Margaret Davidson **$3.50**

☐ NA43868-9 **The Haunting of Grade Three**
   Grace Maccarone **$3.50**

☐ NA40966-2 **Rent a Third Grader** B.B. Hiller **$3.50**

☐ NA41944-7 **The Return of the Third Grade Ghost Hunters**
   Grace Maccarone **$2.99**

☐ NA47463-4 **Second Grade Friends** Miriam Cohen **$3.50**

☐ NA45729-2 **Striped Ice Cream** Joan M. Lexau **$3.50**